For A.J. and Mia Bofinger

D0029026

I SURVIVED

THE WELLINGTON AVALANCHE, 1910

RECEIVED

OCT 15 2022

IDC LIBRARY

NO LONGER PROPERTY OF
THE SEATTLE PUBLIC LIBRARY

by Lauren Tarshis

illustrated by Scott Dawson

Scholastic Inc.

If you purchased this book without a cover, you should be aware that this book is stolen property. It was reported as "unsold and destroyed" to the publisher, and neither the author nor the publisher has received any payment for this "stripped book."

Text copyright © 2022 by Dreyfuss Tarshis Media Inc.
Illustrations copyright © 2022 by Scholastic Inc.

Photos ©: iv: Stefonlinton/Getty Images; 107, 108 top, 108 bottom, 109 top: Skykomish Historical Society Collection; 109 bottom, 110 top: Library of Congress; 110 bottom: Skykomish Historical Society Collection; 115: The Protected Art Archive/Alamy Stock Photo; 119: The Seattle Times; 122, 124 top, 124 bottom: Skykomish Historical Society Collection; 126: University of Washington Libraries, Special Collections, Pickett 3237; 130 top: Granger; 130 center: Association of American Railroads/PhotoQuest/Getty Images; 130 bottom: FLHC 1111/Alamy Stock Photo; 131 top: Bettmann/Getty Images; 131 bottom: Everett Collection Inc./age fotostock; 133: Asar Studios/Alamy Stock Photo; 135: Lysogor Roman/Shutterstock; 136: evenfh/Shutterstock; 137: Tibbut Archive/Alamy Stock Photo.

Special thanks to Martin Burwash.

This book is being published in hardcover by Scholastic Press.

All rights reserved. Published by Scholastic Inc., *Publishers since 1920.* SCHOLASTIC, SCHOLASTIC PRESS, and associated logos are trademarks and/or registered trademarks of Scholastic Inc.

The publisher does not have any control over and does not assume any responsibility for author or third-party websites or their content.

No part of this publication may be reproduced, stored in a retrieval system, or transmitted in any form or by any means, electronic, mechanical, photocopying, recording, or otherwise, without written permission of the publisher. For information regarding permission, write to: Scholastic Inc., Attention: Permissions Department, 557 Broadway, New York, NY 10012.

While inspired by real events and historical characters, this is a work of fiction and does not claim to be historically accurate or to portray factual events or relationships. Please keep in mind that references to actual persons, living or dead, business establishments, events, or locales may not be factually accurate, but rather fictionalized by the author.

ISBN 978-1-338-75256-4

10 9 8 7 6 5 4 3 2 1   22 23 24 25 26

Printed in the U.S.A.   40
First printing 2022
Designed by Katie Fitch

CHAPTER 1

TUESDAY, MARCH 1, 1910
1:40 A.M.
WELLINGTON, WASHINGTON

RRRRRRRooooooooar!

The earsplitting explosion shook the ground. Eleven-year-old Janie Pryor swung her head around and stared in horror. The mountain above her seemed to have shattered apart. A massive wave of icy snow was crashing down.

An avalanche!

For the past six days, Janie had been stuck in this

stormy wilderness. A fierce blizzard had stopped the train she'd been riding, trapping her and dozens of others. Day after day snow gushed from the sky. Icy winds howled. The snow blocked the tracks and practically buried the train. It covered the mountain until even the trees disappeared.

And now Janie was standing outside in the night. Before her eyes, snow had broken loose from the side of the mountain. The thick, white blanket had turned into a churning wave. It sped down the mountain, destroying everything in its path.

Crash!

Trees shattered to bits.

Boom!

Boulders broke loose from the Earth.

With every second the killer wave grew bigger, heavier, deadlier, the snow mixing with wood and rocks and great hunks of dirt. Faster and faster it moved. It was heading right for Janie — and the train with men, women, and children inside. They were all fast asleep. They had no idea what was coming.

"Wake up!" Janie screamed. "Avalanche!"

But the avalanche drowned out her cries.

She took off, running for her life, as the wave of snow thundered after her. Its icy breath huffed behind her. Its frozen jaws snapped at her heels. And suddenly the ground beneath her feet was snatched away. Snow and ice rose up around Janie — and swallowed her whole.

She was part of the wave now, and so was the train. The avalanche had grabbed the cars from the tracks, hurled them into the air like toys. Janie could hear the horrific sounds of the train being torn to shreds. Wood crunching and snapping. Metal screeching. A steam engine hissing like a giant snake.

And people . . . crying out in terror.

Janie's body twisted and spun. Snow lashed at her face and jammed up her nose. She was afraid she'd be torn apart. Until the wave suddenly stopped.

Janie had no idea if she was alive or dead. She couldn't move. She couldn't see or hear. She couldn't breathe.

It seemed that she — and the world — had disappeared.

CHAPTER 2

SEVEN DAYS EARLIER
TUESDAY, FEBRUARY 22, 1910
AROUND 7:00 P.M.
GREAT NORTHERN RAILWAY STATION
SPOKANE, WASHINGTON

Janie sat on a bench in the Great Northern Railway station, scanning the crowd of people waiting for the Seattle train. There were men with thick mustaches and ladies in swishing skirts. A frazzled mother rocked her fussy baby.

Her pigtailed little daughter sat next to her, shrieking, *"Peekaboo!"* at anyone who walked by.

Nobody seemed to notice Janie. And why would they? She'd combed the knots from her hair and scrubbed her nails clean. She had mended the holes in her stockings and shined her boots with spit. She'd made herself look like a normal, respectable eleven-year-old girl.

Nobody would guess that she had a bundle of stolen diamond jewels inside her coat. The glittering rings and earrings were tucked into a secret pocket that rested against Janie's heart.

She glanced across the station at the gorilla-sized man lurking in the corner. He was the one person here who knew what Janie was really doing. Janie didn't know his real name — everyone just called him Hammer. One look at his gigantic fists explained why. He was here to keep an eye on Janie, to make sure she didn't run off with the jewels or get herself into trouble.

When the Seattle train arrived, they'd both get on. Until then, Janie was supposed to sit quietly.

"Don't talk to anyone," Hammer had told her. "Try to disappear."

Janie was good at that — blending in, fading away. And that's what she had been doing. But now she spotted an old lady hobbling along, lugging a giant suitcase. The woman was small and frail and looked like she might keel over. Without thinking, Janie jumped up.

"Ma'am," she said. "May I help you?"

"Aren't you a dear!" the lady said with a kindly smile. "I just need to sit down for a few minutes." Janie took the suitcase and led the lady to a bench.

"There you go," Janie said. She turned to leave, but the lady reached for Janie's arm.

"Sit with me for a few minutes, dear," she said. "I'd like some company."

Janie could feel Hammer's eyes burning into her. Helping old ladies was *not* part of the plan.

But what choice did Janie have?

"I'm Mrs. Letts," the lady said, patting the bench next to her.

Janie sat down.

"Nice to meet you," she said, purposely not saying her own name back. Never tell anyone your real name.

"Are you going to Seattle?" Mrs. Letts asked.

"Yes, ma'am," Janie answered with a fake smile. "I'm visiting my grandma."

A lie.

Janie had no grandma. No mother or father either. They'd both passed away in a motorcar accident when Janie was six. After that, Janie moved from California to live with her aunt Barbara, here in Spokane, Washington. Aunt Barbara wasn't the mothering kind. But at least Janie didn't wind up in an orphanage.

"What a nice girl you are," Mrs. Letts said.

Janie's fake smile wavered. *Nice?* she thought. *What a joke.* If only Mrs. Letts knew the truth: that Janie was a criminal. She worked for the gangster Ray Malvo. Her job was to help get stolen loot out of Spokane.

Tonight her job was to ride the train across the state to Seattle. One of Malvo's goons would

7

be waiting for Janie in an alley behind the train station. She'd hand over the jewels, and he'd give her a bundle of money. Then she'd get back on the train to bring the money home to Malvo.

Malvo. Thinking about him made Janie want to spit. But there was no getting away from him. Just ask Aunt Barbara — she'd been working for Malvo for twenty years.

"I'm heading to Seattle to see my wonderful grandchildren," Mrs. Letts said dreamily. "My grandson is nine," she went on, pulling a photo from her bag and showing it to Janie. "Isn't he handsome?"

Janie's body tingled as she stared at the photo. Something about the kid — the flop of dark hair across his forehead; the small, sparkling eyes. He reminded Janie of her best friend, Dash. Dash was an orphan like Janie, part of Malvo's crew. And like a brother to her.

They used to sneak off together when they weren't working. Their favorite spot was the Spokane Library. They'd made friends with a librarian there, Miss Eva.

She'd sit them in a quiet corner with stacks of books. Sometimes she'd read to them, fairy tales mostly. There was also this story about a little steam engine that has to pull a long and heavy train all the way up a steep mountain. No way can it make it, everyone says. The engine tries. It huffs and puffs. It almost gives up. But then it starts talking to itself.

"I think I can, I think I can!"

It keeps saying those four words, over and over, until finally it makes it to the top.

What a dumb story, Janie had thought. But Dash loved it. He made Miss Eva read it over and over.

Mrs. Letts pulled out a photo of a baby. "And this is my angel . . ."

Janie pretended to admire the photo. But now her mind looped back to the last time she'd seen Dash. It was two months ago, when he came to see her early in the morning.

"I found them!" he'd said breathlessly. "My cousins!"

Dash had always suspected he had family in Boston.

"Miss Eva tracked them down!" he'd told her. "She wrote to them! They sent me a train ticket."

Even now, Janie remembered how she'd felt at that moment. Her heart seemed torn in two. Of course she felt happy for Dash. But how would she live without him by her side?

And then she'd felt a stab of fear.

"What about Malvo?" Janie had gasped. He didn't let anyone quit his crew. His vicious brutes would track Dash down. They'd make sure he never ran — or walked — anywhere again.

"You can't do it!" Janie warned.

"I think I can," Dash said, leaning closer to Janie. "I think I can."

At first Janie couldn't figure out where she'd heard those words before. From that silly train story!

"Dash!" she said. "This isn't a story! This is real life!"

"I know," he said. "But, Janie, maybe it's true. That if you think you can do something —"

They heard Aunt Barbara stomping around. She told Malvo everything — Dash had to go.

Now. Dash grabbed Janie's hand, gripping it hard.

"I'll see you again. I know it!" he said.

And in a blink, he was gone.

Usually Janie managed not to think about Dash. That was something else Janie was good at — not thinking about people. She could push away feelings too, hide them away somewhere deep inside her.

"My stars!" Mrs. Letts exclaimed.

Janie blinked — she'd practically forgotten she was in the train station. Mrs. Letts was pointing at something behind Janie.

Janie whipped around and saw three policemen rushing in through the station door.

She gasped.

They were heading this way, coming right for her!

CHAPTER 3

Janie held her breath as the policemen closed in. She imagined a tiny jail cell, crawling with rats. Murderers all around her. She braced herself — this was the end!

But the policemen rushed right by her.

Janie stared in shock as they surrounded Hammer.

"You're under arrest for the robbery of Drake's Jewelry!" one of the policemen barked, snapping handcuffs onto Hammer's wrists. Janie stood with a small crowd, hoping nobody could hear her heart pounding. She knew what she was supposed to do — wait until the police were gone and then

go directly back to Aunt Barbara's apartment. Malvo would send instructions for what Janie should do next.

Toot! Toot!

The train whistle blared — the Seattle train had arrived. People were heading out to the platform. She gripped her overnight bag, ready to leave the station. But then a shocking idea popped into Janie's mind: *I should still get onto the train.*

Here was her chance to escape this rotten life. Because at this moment, Malvo had no idea that

Hammer had been arrested. And he probably wouldn't find out until sometime tomorrow. Aunt Barbara wasn't expecting Janie home for two days.

Janie's mind spun faster. She could meet up with Malvo's man in Seattle just like she was supposed to. But instead of bringing the money back to Spokane, she'd use it to get away. She could go anywhere.

She could go to Boston and find Dash.

Janie imagined a door opening.

But then it slammed shut.

Don't be a fool, she scolded herself. Malvo would catch her for sure. Bloody thoughts flashed through her mind. Fists. Blades. Cracking bones. She squeezed her eyes to block them out.

Which is why she didn't notice that someone had come up next to her.

"That was amazing!" a voice chimed.

Janie's eyes popped open. A boy was grinning at her. He seemed to be about her age. She quickly looked him up and down. His hair was neatly combed. His coat was fine wool. His boots were brand-new.

Rich kid.

He stepped closer to Janie. "Did you see how the police ran in here? How they arrested that creep? I've never seen anything like it!"

The kid was so excited — you'd think they were at the circus.

He grinned at her. "My name is Frederick McBride," he said. "Are you taking the train to Seattle?"

Janie started to shake her head.

But then a voice whispered to her, like a soft gust of wind.

I think I can.

Her body tensed. Who said that?

She glanced around, but nobody else was near them.

I think I can. I think I can.

Those words, they were in her mind. And they were getting louder. *I think I can.*

The silly train story! Why was she thinking about that now?

And why was she nodding her head?

"Yes," she blurted out. "I'm going to Seattle."

What? No! She couldn't do that!

Just then a tall man strode up to them.

"Frederick, I see you've made yourself a friend," he said, smiling at Janie from under his neatly trimmed gray mustache.

Friend?

"Papa," Frederick said. "This is . . . I'm sorry, what did you say your name was?"

"Janie."

No! She'd said her name! What was wrong with her? She must be under some kind of spell!

"Papa," said Frederick. "Janie is going to Seattle too."

"Very nice, very nice," the man said, peering around. "And where is your family?"

"I'm, uh . . ."

Act normal, she told herself. She didn't want to make them suspicious.

"My parents just dropped me off here," Janie said. "I'm going to visit my grandmother."

"You're traveling all alone?" Mr. McBride said with a worried frown. "It's such a long trip."

"It's just overnight," Janie said. The journey would take about eighteen hours; they'd arrive tomorrow around lunchtime. "I do it all the time. It's Granny's birthday, you see. There's a big party, a surprise . . ."

She was pulling lies out of thin air. But Mr. McBride didn't look convinced.

"Maybe we should speak to the ticket man," he said. "It's just not safe —"

"Papa," Frederick interrupted. "What if Janie rode with us?"

Mr. McBride's face lit up.

"Of course!" he said. "Are you traveling in one of the sleeper cars?"

Sleeper cars! Those were first class.

"No, sir," she said. "I'm in a day coach." That was the cheapest way to travel on a train.

"Not a problem," he said. "I heard the train isn't too crowded. The fellow at the ticket window told me there are only about fifty-five passengers on the whole train tonight. I'll change your ticket. I'm sure there's room. And it would be our great pleasure, young lady."

No, Janie told herself. *Get out now.* She eyed the station door, ready to bolt.

But there was that voice again.

I think I can.

Malvo's face flashed in her mind — his pale, watery eyes. And then Dash's face appeared, with his hopeful smile.

Janie took a breath.

"Thank you, sir," Janie said in her fake cheerful voice. "I'd be very grateful to ride with you."

CHAPTER 4

Janie and Frederick followed Mr. McBride across the train platform, where the Seattle train was waiting. It was freezing cold, and it had started to snow. People hurried across the platform, zig-zagging around workers lugging trunks and boxes. They passed families gripping children and suitcases and a newsboy calling out the headlines.

"Huge blizzard coming to Washington!" he shouted. "Read all about it!"

Janie barely noticed any of it. She still couldn't believe she was going through with this. She kept looking over her shoulder, expecting to see Malvo. Or the police. But nobody was chasing after her. And somehow, she resisted the urge to run.

Mr. McBride strode up to the locomotive, the huge engine car pulling the train. Gray smoke curled from its smokestack, mixing with the icy snowflakes.

"Look at this beauty," he said, patting the engine like it was a prize horse.

It looked way bigger than the engine from that story, strong enough to pull a whole building.

"Steam engines like this changed the world," Mr. McBride said proudly, as if he'd built it himself. He turned to Janie and Frederick. "When I was born, the only way to get to somewhere far away was by horse or boat. It would have taken us months to travel from Spokane to Seattle. And now look at us! This mighty steam engine is going to pull us across the state and over the Cascade Mountains. We're going to get to Seattle in time for lunch tomorrow!"

He looked at the engine again and smiled. "Incredible."

"Papa," Frederick said. "If we don't get on the train, I think we're going to end up *walking* to Seattle."

"Right!" Mr. McBride agreed, giving Frederick's head a playful tap.

As she watched them joking and laughing, Janie's mind flashed to a man with bright eyes and a gentle smile — her own papa. And Mama, with her shiny curls and chiming laugh. And the grinning, carefree face of a little girl . . . Janie.

Janie took a sharp breath and swallowed hard. She blinked her eyes — and Mama and Papa were gone.

Frederick talked nonstop as they hurried alongside the train, away from the locomotive.

"Looks like there are seven cars on the train," he said, pointing out the baggage car, the mail car, and two second-class day coaches. "There's an observation car at the very back. That's my favorite car, where people go to sit when they're not in one of the two sleeper cars. I'll show it to you."

Janie nodded politely, but her skin was prickling. This kid really thought they were buddies, she realized. She was going to have to spend time with him on the train. She'd have to hold on to this nice-girl act, keep careful track of her lies so she didn't get caught.

Their first-class sleeper car was near the very back of the train. It was painted shiny maroon.

"Welcome!" said a smiling man in a blue uniform, who stood at the door. "I'm Mr. Anderson. I'll be your porter for this trip. If you need anything at all, you let me know."

"Thank you, sir!" Mr. McBride said, stepping aside so Janie could go first. She hesitated for a split second — this was her last chance. And then she climbed aboard.

Janie stared in amazement at their sleeper car. The polished wooden walls gleamed. The seats were plush red velvet. Flickering brass lamps filled the car with a golden light. It was like the lobby of the Pennington Hotel, the best in Spokane. That's where Malvo sent kids to pick pockets and steal purses.

It even smelled good — like perfume and cigars. Now Janie understood why the first-class cars were way in the back of the train. That way the richest passengers didn't have to breathe in the stinking, choking smoke from the locomotive. On her last train trip, the smoke in the day coach was so thick it burned her throat. When she blew her nose, her snot was pitch-black.

They walked through the narrow aisle.

"Well, hello, dear!" said Mrs. Letts from the first row.

Janie forced a smile.

In the next row was a young woman writing furiously in a notebook. From behind her seat, a freckled face popped up. It was the pesty little girl from the station.

"Peekaboo!" the little girl shrieked, grinning at Janie. She jumped up and down like a crazed kangaroo.

"Violet, sit down," said her mother as she tried to calm her fussing baby boy.

"Peekaboo, I see you!" Violet said again.

"I think she likes you," Frederick said to Janie.

Janie hoped not. Little kids were trouble. Once they got attached, there was no shaking them loose.

"Here we are," Mr. McBride said, pointing to two big seats across from each other.

"The beds are hidden in the ceiling," Frederick said, pointing up. "The porter, Mr. Anderson, will come through later and take them down for us. They're really comfortable. Curtains come down in front so you feel like you have a private room."

Dash would love this! Janie thought.

Mr. McBride and Frederick stowed their fine leather suitcases under their seat. Janie did the same with her frayed canvas bag. She had nothing to sleep in, she realized. Nobody wore pajamas in the day coaches. All she had in her bag were some clean underclothes and a pair of red knee socks. She guessed it didn't matter. She wasn't planning to actually sleep tonight. She had to stay awake and on guard.

"May I hang your coat for you?" Mr. McBride said, holding out his hand.

"No, thank you," Janie said quickly, taking a step back. She couldn't let her coat — or the diamond jewels hidden in that chest pocket — out of her sight. "I'm a little chilly."

The train whistle shrieked.

Whooooooooooooooooooo! Whooooooooooooooo!

A man's voice shouted out: "All aboard! Train Twenty-Five, the Seattle Express!"

"Here we go," Frederick said.

Janie sat down in her seat as the train gave a shudder and started to move.

Slowly at first.

Chuuuuugga . . . chuuuuugga . . . chuuuuugga.

Then faster.

CHUggachuggachuggachugga.

CHUggachuggachuggachugga . . .

Janie looked out the window. It was snowing harder now. The station lights twinkled through the white swirl and then disappeared as the train picked up speed.

There was no turning back now.

CHAPTER 5

LATER THAT NIGHT
AROUND 8:30 P.M.

"Come on," Frederick said to Janie. "We're going to the observation car."

"No, thank you," Janie said politely. "You don't need to worry about me."

What she needed to do was lie low, try to disappear until the train arrived in Seattle. But Frederick and Mr. McBride weren't going to let her out of their sight.

"You're with us, my dear!" Mr. McBride said.

Janie's heart sank — what choice did she have? She was supposed to be a girl with good manners. Mr. McBride had paid for her to ride first class. It would be rude to refuse the invitation.

The observation car was just behind their sleeper car. There were big chairs along the windows and tables where some men were playing cards. They found some seats and Mr. McBride quickly made friends with two other passengers.

One was Mr. Riggins, a bald-headed man with a booming voice and a walrus mustache. The other was the young lady with the notebook that Janie had seen when she first got onto the train. Her name was Libby Wade. She was from Minneapolis, and it turned out she was a writer.

"If I may ask," Mr. McBride said. "What are you writing about?"

"This train trip," answered Miss Wade. "A journey west on the Great Northern Railway."

She explained that she'd already traveled more than a thousand miles, through Minnesota, North Dakota, Montana, and Idaho. This

stretch — three hundred and fifty miles across Washington State — was the last part of the trip.

"Wonderful," Mr. McBride said, with the same proud look he'd had when he admired the big locomotive. "Of all the railroads, the Great Northern is my favorite. Everything is tip-top."

"Always on time, and the cars are spotless," Mr. Riggins agreed. "Never any surprises."

Miss Wade nodded, but her smile wavered. "That's the problem. Nothing exciting has happened on this trip."

If only she knew, Janie thought.

"I'm afraid this article is shaping up to be a dud," Miss Wade added.

"But what about meeting us?" Frederick asked with a big, joking grin.

Everyone chuckled, and Janie fake-smiled along.

"Well, of course," Miss Wade said. "That's the best part of being on a train — meeting interesting people."

"I met my dear wife on a train," Mr. McBride said.

Janie pictured Frederick's mother — some rich lady dripping in jewels and silk, Janie was sure. She'd overheard Mr. McBride telling the others that he was a banker and that the family lived in Seattle. Probably in a huge palace.

"But, Miss Wade, this trip isn't over yet!" Frederick said.

"The young man is correct." Mr. Riggins nodded. "In fact, for us it's just beginning. Maybe something exciting is yet to come."

Miss Wade sighed. "I'm afraid not," she said.

"We'll go to sleep soon. And when we wake up, we'll practically be in Seattle."

Thank goodness for that, Janie thought.

"But wait!" Frederick exclaimed. "I know what you can write about." He leaned forward. "That jewel thief!"

The blood drained from Janie's face.

"What jewel thief?" Miss Wade asked.

"A man was arrested in the train station, just before the train left," Mr. McBride explained. "You must have already been on the train platform."

"He robbed a jewelry store in Spokane!" Frederick went on. "He must have been trying to escape on the train. But the police caught him. They surrounded the guy, put handcuffs on him, and dragged him out."

"It was something," Mr. Riggins said. "The fellow looked like a real lowlife."

Janie's stomach twisted into such a tight knot she was afraid she'd puke.

"How terrible," Miss Wade said.

"It all happened so quickly," Mr. McBride added.

"I've been thinking about that guy," Frederick said, his eyes narrowing. "I knew there was something suspicious about him even before the police showed up."

"Why is that?" Miss Wade asked.

Frederick shrugged.

"He had this sneaky look in his eye. He was watching everyone. And there's something else — That guy wasn't working alone. He kept looking around. I'm pretty sure there was someone else at the station with him. Another crook who got away."

Janie's mouth dropped open, but she quickly closed it.

"So you think there's a jewel thief on the loose?" Mr. Riggins asked.

"Not only that," Frederick said. "I think that dirty criminal could be right here on this train!"

CHAPTER 6

This is it, Janie thought. Frederick knew it was her! She expected him to leap to his feet and point at Janie. "It's you!" he'd shout.

But Frederick just sat there. And Mr. McBride let out a little chuckle.

"I think someone's been reading a few too many mystery stories," he said, giving Frederick's arm a gentle pat.

"You have a wonderful imagination," Miss Wade said kindly.

Janie exhaled; she hadn't realized she'd been holding her breath.

Mr. Anderson appeared.

"I've made down your beds for you all," he said. "You can come whenever you're ready."

Janie kept the fake smile glued to her face as they walked back to the sleeper car. The beds were all set up. Long green curtains hung in front of each bed, so people could sleep without anyone watching them. The little girl, Violet, skipped through the aisle in her flowered nightgown and slippers.

"Nighty! Night! Janie!" Violet shrieked, spinning around and skipping back to her bed.

How had she learned Janie's name?

"She *definitely* likes you," Frederick laughed.

"She's adorable!" Janie gushed, as she groaned inside.

Finally, Janie climbed into her bed and closed the curtains. Frederick was right; it really did seem to be her own private room. And what a bed! There were two fluffy pillows, soft sheets that smelled like flowers, and a thick wool blanket. It was nothing like where Janie slept at Aunt Barbara's, on a lumpy mattress with just a raggedy quilt to keep her from shivering to death.

She settled herself back, sighing softly with relief. She rubbed her aching cheeks. Who knew fake-smiling could hurt so much? What a relief to be alone, to go back to being her regular self.

She'd made it through the evening. Like Miss Wade had said, they'd be in Seattle soon. Janie would lose Mr. McBride and Frederick in the Seattle station. Then she'd find Malvo's goon in the alley, get the money, and buy herself a ticket for a train heading east. Excitement shimmered inside her. By tomorrow night she'd be free.

She took off her boots and shrugged off her coat. She checked that the diamond jewels were safe in the hidden pocket, folded the coat, and put it under her pillows.

Usually, Janie stayed up all night when she rode a train. But soon she was snuggled under the sweet-smelling sheets, cozy under the thick blanket. The train swayed gently back and forth. The sound of the train was like a song.

Chuggachuggachugga.

Chuggachuggachugga.

Chuggachuggachugga.

34

She tried to keep her eyes open, but she'd soon drifted into a sound sleep. The next thing she knew, it was morning.

She sat up and looked around. Where *was* she?

The train! She'd slept through the entire night!

She thrust her hand under her pillows. Her coat was there — the jewels were safe.

But wait . . .

Something was wrong.

The train was silent. And they weren't moving.

Were they already in Seattle?

No. Mr. Anderson would have made sure they were all awake.

She peeled back the shade that covered the window next to her bed. Snow poured down in thick sheets. It was impossible to see where they were.

Voices sounded from the other side of her curtains.

"Where are we?"

"Why have we stopped?"

A man's voice rose up.

"There's been an avalanche!"

CHAPTER 7

LATER THAT MORNING
WEDNESDAY, FEBRUARY 25
AROUND 8:00 A.M.

Janie stood in the aisle with Frederick and the other bleary-eyed passengers. Most were still in their pajamas and robes, their hair rumpled from sleep. The train's conductor, Mr. Pettit, had come to their car to explain what had happened.

"It's nothing serious," he said in a jolly voice. "The train will be moving very soon."

"Someone said there was a . . . an *avalanche*?" Mrs. Letts said.

"That's just another word for snowslide," Mr. Pettit said. "In the winter up here in the mountains, snow can slide off slopes and onto the tracks. It happens all the time on this part of our Great Northern rail line."

"I've never heard that," Mr. Riggins muttered.

"And as I said, it's nothing to be concerned about," Mr. Pettit continued. "Because the Great Northern Railway has a snow-fighting army already at work — three hundred men to shovel snow. And we have five of the most powerful snowplows on Earth."

"But, sir," asked Miss Wade. "Where exactly are we?"

"In the mountains," Mr. Pettit said. "We're in a little railroad town called Cascade, about eighty-five miles from Seattle. We're right at the entrance to the Cascade Tunnel."

"So the middle of nowhere," Mr. Riggins grumbled.

Janie flashed in her mind to the atlas in the library. She and Dash always loved looking at the different maps in that big, heavy book. She pictured the map of Washington State — a rectangle way up at the top left corner of the United States. The city of Spokane was on one side of the rectangle — the right side. Straight across the state on the other side was Seattle. In between? Lots of empty green. Squiggles of rivers. And the jagged lines of the Cascade Mountains.

This train was trapped inside those jagged lines.

The middle of nowhere was right!

Frederick eyed Miss Wade.

"Now you'll have something to write about in your article!"

She smiled a little. "That's true," she said. "But I'm not sure this is what I had in mind."

"How long will we be stopped here?" Mrs. Letts asked, pulling her thick pink robe more tightly around her shoulders. "My grandchildren are waiting for me."

"We should get to Seattle sometime around midnight," Mr. Pettit said.

"Tonight!" Mr. Riggins snapped. "That's more than twelve hours late!"

Twelve hours?

A clock began to tick inside Janie's skull.

Tick, tick, tick, tick . . .

By early this afternoon, someone would call Malvo to say that Hammer was arrested.

Tick, tick, tick, tick . . .

He'd call Aunt Barbara, who'd tell him that Janie hadn't come home.

Tick, tick, tick, tick . . .

"Ladies and gentlemen, there is some good news," Mr. Pettit said. "Just a short walk from the train tracks is the best railroad cookhouse in the West — we call it the beanery. So, everyone, bundle up and get ready for the most delicious pancakes you've ever tasted."

"I love pancakes!" Violet cheered.

She scooted over to Janie and bounced up and down. "Janie! Janie! Pancakes! Pancakes!"

But all Janie heard was *tick, tick, tick, tick.*

She looked out the window and imagined Malvo's face — his thick, unsmiling lips. It

CANADA

Wellington

Cascade

Scenic

Seattle

CASCADE RANGE

WASHINGTON

PACIFIC OCEAN

OREGON

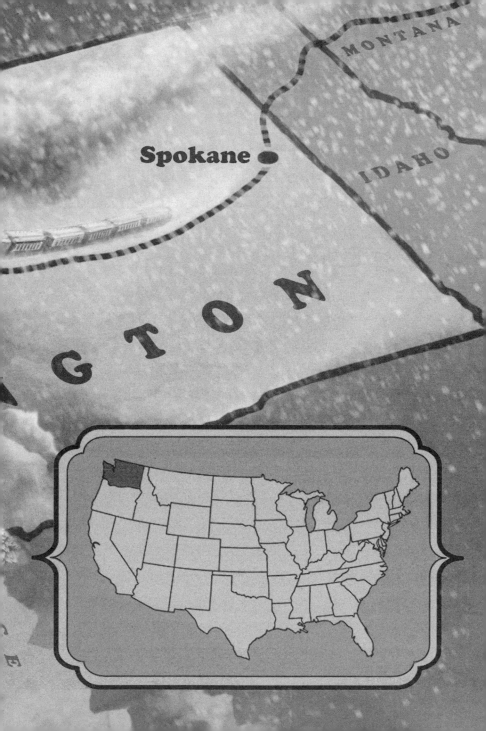

wouldn't take him long to figure out that Janie had gotten on the train. That she planned to run away . . . with the jewels.

Janie's guts twisted. Blood pounded in her ears.

What had given her the idea that she could escape from Malvo? She'd made a huge mistake! And now there was nothing she could do.

She was trapped.

CHAPTER 8

LATER WEDNESDAY MORNING
CASCADE, WASHINGTON

Stepping out of the train car, all Janie could see was snow. It gushed from the sky, big fat flakes that stuck to her coat sleeves like glue. Drifts rose up higher than Janie's head. Luckily, there was a shoveled path that led from the train to the beanery.

Snow blew across Janie's face. But she managed to catch glimpses of the town around them. If you could even call it a town.

There were no roads or stores, no proper houses or brick-and-stone buildings like in Spokane. Definitely no library. Most of the little wooden buildings were crowded along the railroad tracks. Up the hill was a scattering of sad-looking cottages and shacks. Mountains jutted up around them.

"What a terrible place," Mr. Riggins mumbled as they trudged along.

It was grim. But no worse than the dark little apartment where she lived with Aunt Barbara, with stray dogs howling from the trash-filled alley below.

They were all half-frozen when they stumbled into the beanery. It was just a large room with grimy floors and walls that shook with every gust of wind. But a glowing fire crackled in a big potbellied stove, and the smell of pancakes and syrup filled the air.

"Now this is worth writing about!" Miss Wade said excitedly.

The long tables and benches were already crowded with other passengers. Janie didn't

44

recognize most of them — they must have been passengers from the other sleeper and the day coaches.

She waved at Mrs. Letts and Violet's mom — her name was Mrs. Kayden. She was bouncing her baby boy on her knee. He flashed a gummy grin at anyone who looked his way. Janie couldn't see Violet, but she knew the little pest was here somewhere.

And sure enough, just as they all sat down at a long table, the little girl popped up right next to Janie.

"*Peekaboo*, Janie!"

"Violet!" called her mother. "Come back over here. I told you not to wander away!"

Violet leaned close to Janie, sending her syrup breath into Janie's face.

"I'm going to build a snowman," she whispered. Then she darted away.

Just then, a thick-bearded man in an apron appeared at their table. He was carrying two trays loaded with food.

"Hope you folks are hungry." He grinned.

"Smells good," said Mr. Riggins, perking up at the sight of pancakes, eggs, and sausages.

Miss Wade flipped open her notebook. She plucked a pencil from behind her ear.

"Are you the chef here?" she asked the bearded man.

"Just the waiter," he said. "The name's John. There's our cook, Harry, right over there."

He pointed to a tall man standing behind a huge cookstove. The man looked over with a welcoming smile and a big wave.

"It's very generous of you two, to feed us all," Mr. McBride said.

"It's a big crowd," he said. "We've got the passengers and crew from your train, plus eight more men from the mail train."

"Mail train?" Mr. Riggins asked.

"It arrived here a few hours after your train. Stuck here too."

Everyone piled their plates high. But Janie's stomach was still twisting and churning. She couldn't even think of eating. Glancing up at the windows, she kept imagining Malvo's face.

She shrunk down on the bench. If only she really could disappear, like a wizard in one of Miss Eva's fairy tales.

Groups of passengers came and went. Each time the door opened, the wind sent napkins flying and snowflakes swirling through the air.

"Quite a blizzard out there," Mr. McBride said as John poured coffee from a battered tin pot.

"I'll say," John said. "We get more snow up here than almost anywhere in the whole country. And this blizzard is one of the worst I've seen in my many years here. Yesterday we got ten feet of snow — maybe more. Trains are stuck up and down the line. Telegraph service is knocked out. Telephones too. All over the state."

Janie's ears pricked up.

"Nobody can send a message?" she asked. "Or call anyone?"

Everyone looked at her; she'd barely said a word since they'd left Spokane.

"That's right," John said. "And not just here. Blizzards are slamming half the country. Everything is shut down."

"I'm sure your family in Seattle knows the train is delayed," Mr. McBride said to Janie.

Janie nodded and tried to·look worried. But inside she was cheering.

Malvo had no way of finding out that Hammer had been arrested. Maybe her plan wasn't ruined! And even if it was, she'd have more time to make a new one.

She sat up straighter. The ticking in her mind stopped. For now, at least, she was safe.

She eyed the pancakes and put two onto her plate. Suddenly she was starving. Frederick handed her the pitcher of syrup.

But she'd barely taken a bite when worried voices erupted from the other end of the table.

"Violet? Violet?"

"Where is she?"

"I don't see her anywhere."

"What's happened?" Miss Wade called out.

"My little girl!" cried Mrs. Kayden. "She's gone!"

CHAPTER 9

In a blink, everyone in the beanery seemed to be on their feet. Janie leapt up and joined the search. People raced around the little shack, calling for Violet. They searched under tables, behind barrels, in dusty corners. But there was no sign of the little girl.

Suddenly, Janie remembered what Violet had whispered to her: *I'm going to build a snowman.*

"She's outside!" Janie shouted, racing toward the door.

"No, she couldn't have gotten out!" Mrs. Kayden gasped.

But, of course, Janie knew how easy it was to slip away when no one was looking. To disappear. With so many people coming in and out of the beanery, Violet could have snuck outside without anyone noticing.

Without even thinking, Janie opened the door and plunged into the blizzard.

Frederick, Mr. McBride, and Miss Wade rushed out after her, along with John and some others.

"Violet!" they called. "Violet!"

Only the wind and snow answered them.

The cold drilled through Janie's thin wool coat and up through the patched holes in her flimsy boots. Her bones seemed to freeze.

Nobody would last long out here, she thought. *Especially not a little kid.* Janie thought of those many freezing nights she'd spent shivering behind buildings, hiding out from the police. How her hands would get numb. How her teeth would chatter so hard she was afraid they'd crumble to dust.

"Violet!" she hollered, as loudly as she could. "Violet!"

She heard a sound, like a cat mewing. But no

cat would be out here in the snow. Janie listened more closely. She narrowed her eyes, peering through the swirling snow the way she scanned the streets of Spokane for police and stray dogs. But all she saw were snowdrifts.

Until . . . one of the snowdrifts seemed to move. Janie lurched forward and thrust her arms into the snow. She felt a warm body.

Violet!

Janie lifted the shivering little girl out of the snow and held her tight.

"Janie found Violet!" Frederick shouted, punching his fist in the air.

"Brava!" cheered Miss Wade.

Janie smiled — a real smile. The first one since Dash left.

They warmed Violet up in front of the crackling fire. Her mother had peeled off her soaking dress. Harry, the chef, had found a thick flannel shirt for Violet to wear and a blanket to wrap around her. Pretty soon the little girl was smiling and back to her bossy self.

"I want more pancakes!" she demanded, climbing on Janie's lap.

"I just cleaned the grill," Harry said. "But for you, sweetheart, I'll fire it up again."

"Thank you," Mrs. Kayden said gratefully. "But I'm going to take Violet back to the train." Her baby boy had started to yowl. "Poor little Billy is exhausted. He needs a nap."

"Go, Mommy!" Violet commanded. "I stay with Janie!"

Miss Wade put a hand on little Billy's bald

head. "Take the baby down to the train. We can keep an eye on Violet here."

After Mrs. Kayden left, Violet devoured a stack of pancakes. When she was finished, she let out a little burp, curled up against Janie's chest, and fell asleep.

Harry stepped away from the grill, took off his apron, and plopped himself down on a stool.

"I'm ready for *my* nap!" he said, rubbing his hands through his shaggy beard. "We've been working since three o'clock this morning."

"You'll have some peace and quiet soon," Mr. McBride said with his usual smile. "Our train will be leaving in the next hour or two."

Harry's eyebrows slid up. "Who told you that?"

"The conductor. Mr. Pettit," said Mr. Riggins. "He's a good chap."

"He is," Harry said. "One of the best on the Great Northern line. But I'm afraid he's dead wrong. Your train isn't going anywhere today. Probably not tomorrow either."

"But we were told the tracks were just about cleared," Mr. McBride said with surprise.

Harry shook his head. "There are slides happening up and down the line. The snowplows can't keep up, and there aren't nearly enough shovelers."

"Seems you folks are stuck with us," John said.

Mr. Riggins muttered a bad word under his breath. But Janie almost smiled. The longer the blizzard lasted, the more time she had to make her plan.

"Lucky you're here in Cascade," Harry said. "You could be stranded out there in the middle of the mountains."

"Oh my," Miss Wade said. "I hadn't even thought of that possibility."

"It happens," John said. "Just a few years ago, in 1907, there was a train like yours that got stranded. They were stuck for ten days."

"Ten days!" Mr. Riggins exclaimed.

"The snow was coming down so fast," John continued. "The plows and shovelers couldn't get to the train."

"They ran out of coal," Harry said. "Couldn't run the heaters."

"What about food?" Mr. McBride asked.

"They did have a dining car, unlike your train," Harry continued. "But that food ran out very quickly. I imagine people were starving."

"That train must have stunk!" Frederick said. "Where did everyone . . . you know . . ."

"Frederick," Mr. McBride warned.

But Janie understood. The toilet rooms in their sleeper car already smelled terrible.

"I don't know about that," Harry said. "But things must have been mighty bad. Because passengers gave up waiting to be rescued. They left the train and walked five miles along the snowy tracks, until they got to a town."

"Walked? In a blizzard?" Mr. McBride said, his eyes wide.

"That's right," Harry said. "It's a miracle they all made it back, that nobody froze or got buried by a slide."

"Don't forget the grizzly bears that live up here . . . and bobcats," John said with a shudder. "Wolves too. I wouldn't head out there for all the money in the world."

"And good thing we don't have to," Mr. McBride said.

Just then, Violet woke up. She rubbed her face against the front of Janie's coat.

Then her head snapped back.

"Ouch!" she cried.

She looked up at Janie with teary eyes. There was a long scratch on her cheek, oozing blood.

"What happened?" Frederick said as Harry rushed to get a clean rag.

Miss Wade leaned close to Violet. "Oh, it's just a little scratch," she said with relief, lifting Violet from Janie's lap. "She must have nicked herself outside in the snow."

Janie glanced down. To her horror, she saw a tiny, sparkling point poking out through the front of her coat.

It was part of a diamond.

CHAPTER 10

Janie's heart was still hammering when they got back to the train. She grabbed her overnight bag from under her seat and went into the washroom. She locked the door and took off her coat. Inside the coat's lining, the hidden pocket was fraying; stitches had come loose. That's how one of the rings had wormed its way through the thin wool of Janie's coat.

Luckily, Violet wasn't really hurt — and nobody had noticed the glittering speck on Janie's coat. She'd quickly pushed it back through the little hole.

Still, it was a close call. And now Janie had to figure out what to do with the jewels.

Janie carefully dug them out of the hidden pocket. She held the glittering bundle in her hand.

"Janie! Janie!"

Little fists pounded on the door.

"Just a minute, Violet!"

Janie sighed. Little kids were the worst. Even cute ones like Violet.

She quickly pulled a long red wool sock from her bag. She stuffed the jewels into the toe, rolled the sock into a tight ball, and tucked it into the bottom of her bag. It wasn't the best hiding place. But it would have to do.

That entire day and night passed. And the next day was more of the same — waiting, meals at the beanery, cards and checkers to pass the time. They did finally see two snowplows in action. They were massive, pushed by giant locomotives. Passengers pressed their faces to the windows as the plows cleared away snow that blocked their train.

But it was no use. The snow kept coming, and within a few hours the track was hopelessly blocked again.

"My family must be so worried!"

"I'm going to get fired from my job!"

By that night rumors were swirling about the five snowplows on the mountain — that at least one of them had broken down, and that the four others were running low on coal. They also heard that many of the shovelers were exhausted and couldn't keep up with the snow pouring down.

Poor Mrs. Letts stared teary-eyed at the photos of her grandchildren. Violet was bouncing off the walls. She kept begging to build a snowman, but the gushing snow and fierce winds wouldn't let up.

But nobody was more upset than Mr. Riggins. All Thursday he paced the aisles, checking his pocket watch. He pestered Mr. Pettit for updates.

Finally, after supper that night, the conductor had news.

"We're leaving Cascade tonight," he announced. "And —"

Cheers filled the car.

"Just a moment," Mr. Pettit called, holding out his hands for people to hush up. "We're not going to Seattle. We're moving to the other side of the tunnel, to a town called Wellington. It's just a short ride, about three miles. We'll be staying in Wellington until, uh . . . the tracks are clear."

The cheers turned to groans.

"Why leave Cascade if we're only going three miles?" Mr. McBride asked.

"The beanery is running low on food," Mr. Pettit said. "But there's plenty for us in Wellington. Coal too. Now if you'll excuse me . . ."

He turned to leave, but Mr. Riggins blocked his way.

"I demand the truth!" he said, his cheeks beet red. "When will this train get to Seattle?"

The conductor's shoulders slumped a bit. Janie could see how exhausted he was.

"At this point, I just don't know," he said. "This blizzard . . . it's very bad."

He said a polite goodbye and headed out of their car, leaving a trail of complaints behind him.

Late that night, the train moved through the pitch-black tunnel. It wasn't until Friday morning that they got a look at Wellington. It was a little railroad town like Cascade, just a bunch of roughly built shacks and cottages scattered like freckles around a railyard.

What was different here was that this tiny town seemed to be hanging off the side of the mountain. Their train was parked on the edge of a skinny ledge — overlooking a canyon.

"I didn't think it was possible," said Mr. Riggins as they trudged along a shoveled path to get breakfast. "But this place is even more of a dump than Cascade."

Frederick turned to Janie and rolled his eyes. Everyone was getting tired of Mr. Riggins's griping.

But even Mr. Riggins cheered up a bit when he saw where they'd be eating their meals. It was a hotel called Bailets. The rough, rambling white building was nothing fancy like the Pennington in Spokane. Compared to the beanery, though, Bailets was fit for kings and queens.

The tables were covered with blue-and-red checked tablecloths. There were plants hanging in front of the big windows. The owners, Mr. and Mrs. Bailets, weren't as friendly as Harry and John, and there were no pancakes. But Janie devoured her plate of sausages and eggs. There was even dessert — pears in syrup.

Janie had just swallowed the last sweet bite when the dining room door flew open. A young man staggered in. He wore tattered work clothes. Icicles hung from his tangled beard, and he had a bloody bandage dangling from his head. Janie saw right away that he wasn't from their train.

Mrs. Bailets leapt up to help him through the door.

"I've come from Cascade," the man rasped. "I walked through the tunnel. I just had to get out . . ."

Someone grabbed a chair for the man, and Mrs. Bailets wrapped a blanket around him.

"There was an avalanche," he said, his voice quavering. "A monster avalanche. It took everything . . ."

Gasps filled the dining room.

"It happened early this morning, before dawn," the man stammered on. "I heard a terrible sound. At first, I thought it was trains coming. But it was louder than that — I never heard such a sound."

The man looked around with wild eyes. Janie's palms started to sweat. She wasn't sure if she wanted to hear what came next.

"I looked up and it seemed like the entire mountain was breaking apart. The snow came down so fast. There were trees, boulders . . ."

More gasps rang out, and a few sobs.

"I managed to dive out of the way just in time," the young man said. "But the slide smashed right into the beanery. Crushed it! There's nothing left."

Nobody spoke for a moment, until Miss Wade asked the question on everyone's minds.

"What about Harry and John?"

Janie pictured those kind and friendly men who had fed them in Cascade, who had taken such good care of Violet after Janie found her in the snow.

The young man's shoulders slumped.

"We dug for hours." His voice cracked. "And when we found them . . ." He gulped and closed his eyes.

"It was too late. Those two good men . . . they're dead."

CHAPTER 11

```
THE NEXT MORNING
SATURDAY, FEBRUARY 26
AROUND 9:00 A.M.
BAILETS DINING ROOM
WELLINGTON, WASHINGTON
```

Clink clink clink. Mr. Riggins nervously tapped his fork on his plate. Janie, Frederick, Mr. Riggins, Mr. McBride, and Miss Wade were at their usual table at Bailets, eating breakfast.

"The same thing that happened in Cascade could happen here," Mr. Riggins said grimly.

65

"You can see how the snow is piling up on the side of the mountain. It's all hanging over us. All it would take —"

"Mr. Riggins, please," Miss Wade said sharply, cutting Mr. Riggins off and flicking her eyes toward Janie and Frederick.

"Could a big avalanche happen here?" Frederick asked worriedly.

The hairs on Janie's neck stood up. But Mr. McBride quickly calmed her fears.

"We are perfectly safe," he said, without a shred of doubt. "Mr. Bailets told me that avalanches have always been a problem in Cascade. But not here in Wellington. The slope of the mountain is different. He says there has never been an avalanche here."

"And he should know," said Miss Wade, picking up her coffee mug. "He and his wife have lived here for twenty years —"

"No!" Mr. Riggins said, suddenly standing up. He marched over to the window.

"I've made up my mind. We should leave here. As soon as possible!" He turned back toward the table.

"I've spoken to some of the workers. The town of Scenic is only about five miles from here. All we have to do is follow the tracks. We'll see a trail that leads down the mountain, straight into the town."

Mr. McBride stared at him. "You're saying we should walk five miles across these mountains, in a blizzard? I'm sorry, my friend, but that's ridiculous."

Angry red splotches appeared on Mr. Riggins's cheeks.

"You're not thinking clearly," Mr. McBride went on. "This blizzard will be over soon. Mr. Pettit says —"

"Pettit has no idea what's happening!" Mr. Riggins snapped, pounding his fist on their table. A fork clattered to the floor. "Don't you see? We're like those passengers on the train that was stranded in 1907. We're on our own. If we want to get out of here, we're going to have to walk. Because if we don't get out of here soon . . ."

"Mr. Riggins —" Miss Wade said.

"I'm leaving tomorrow morning," he said. "With or without you all."

And with a last huff of anger, he stormed away.

"He'll never do it," Mr. McBride said, reaching down and picking up the dropped fork.

But Mr. Riggins left early the next morning, taking three other men with him. All day, people worried about what could happen to them.

"They could fall off a cliff!"

"I hear there are packs of hungry wolves out there."

"If they're buried in a slide, we won't find them until spring."

The mood on the train got gloomier and gloomier with each passing hour. And not only because people were worried about Mr. Riggins and the other men. Snow was piling up on the mountain. Food was running low at Bailets; dinner that night was greasy potatoes and bitter fried onions.

Adding to the worries, the train was out of fresh water. Mr. Anderson was melting snow so they had water to drink. But there wasn't much for washing up. No wonder the train stunk so bad, like sweaty bodies and dirty diapers.

Nobody ate much at breakfast Monday morning. Janie picked at her plate of greasy potatoes.

Their little group was getting ready to head back to the train when four men stumbled in through the dining room door.

They looked half-frozen, with beards caked with snow. Each carried a big shovel.

"That's our army of shovelers?" Miss Wade whispered, lifting her eyebrows. "Poor things."

"We've come from Scenic," called out a tall man with a bright red nose. "Is Mr. Bailets here? We have a message, about some men from your train."

Frederick looked at Janie with wide eyes.

"It's about Mr. Riggins!" he said.

The red-nosed man reached into his pocket and took out a piece of paper. He handed it to Mr. Bailets.

Mrs. Letts's hands flew to her heart. "Oh dear," she gasped.

The dining room fell silent, and all eyes were on Mr. Bailets as he unfolded the paper.

Janie braced herself for terrible news.

CHAPTER 12

Mr. Bailets looked up from the note, and a smile burst onto his face.

"They made it to Scenic! And by later today they'll all be on a train back to Seattle."

Happy shouts bubbled up through the dining room, and relief washed over Janie. She hadn't realized how worried she'd been.

"But Riggins warns that others should not try to walk to Scenic," Mr. Bailets went on. "Says it's too dangerous."

The red-nosed man nodded. "I'd never do it again."

"We almost got buried in a slide coming here," said a tall man in a ragged coat, his voice raspy with fear. "Thought we were done for."

Stay or go? Stay or go? That's all anyone was talking about in the observation car that afternoon.

Janie and Frederick listened in as they played their one hundredth game of checkers.

"I'd leave this train if I could," Mrs. Letts said. "But I wouldn't make it very far. And what about people with young children, like Mrs. Kayden? How could she manage, hiking through a blizzard with Violet and the baby?"

They'd never make it, Janie thought.

"You're safer here," Mr. McBride assured Mrs. Letts.

"We all are," Miss Wade agreed.

Frederick and Janie went on with their game. Frederick was winning, and he was studying the board closely. But then he suddenly looked up at Janie.

"I . . . I know it sounds odd," he said quietly.

"But I kind of like being stuck out here, away from school — from everything."

Janie flinched as she suddenly thought of what might be waiting for her in Seattle. Malvo's goons. The police. More cold nights hiding in filthy alleys. Up here in the middle of nowhere, Janie hadn't thought of any of that. Part of her definitely wished this blizzard would never end.

"Me too," she said to Frederick.

But why wouldn't Frederick want to go back home? Janie figured his life was perfect in Seattle, like a prince in one of Miss Eva's fairy tales.

"I miss my mom and everything," Frederick said, as though he'd read Janie's mind. "But at home I barely ever see my father. He's always so busy. And, well . . ." He looked up at Janie. "It's fun to make a new friend."

A friend? Janie couldn't stop herself from smiling.

"For me, too," Janie said. And to her surprise, she realized she wasn't lying.

Frederick was about to win Janie's last checker when Violet appeared. She was bright-eyed from her nap. She raced over to them, bumping the table and scattering the checkers into a jumble.

"No!" Frederick laughed. "I was about to win!"

"Don't be so sure," Janie joked, picking Violet up and plopping her on her lap.

"I want to build my snowman!" Violet said. Again.

"Actually, the weather isn't so bad right now," Frederick said, glancing out the window. It had warmed up overnight. For a few hours, the snow had actually turned to rain. It was snowing again now, but not too hard.

"Let's go," Janie said.

They bundled Violet up and took her outside. Frederick found a shovel and they got to work. Soon three other kids from the day cars joined them. They threw snowballs and climbed the drifts. Miss Wade came outside to watch, and Mrs. Kayden brought baby Billy. Happy giggles echoed through the mountains.

When they'd finished the snowman, Mr. Anderson brought them two pieces of coal for eyes. Miss Wade plopped her green feathered hat onto the snowman's bald head.

"Very elegant," Mrs. Kayden laughed. "Now let's get inside."

Violet was sopping wet, and Billy was fussing.

"But snowman needs a scarf!" Violet cried.

"She's right," Frederick said, looking around.

"We'll find one later," Janie said, picking the little girl up.

They climbed back onto the sleeper car, which was empty. Voices echoed from the observation car next door.

"Everyone must be in there," Frederick said.

They left Violet with her mother in the observation car. Then they went back to their sleeper car and Janie visited the washroom, holding her nose against the stench.

When she came out, she was surprised to see her overnight bag sitting out on the seat, unzipped. That was not where she'd left it.

Dread crept up her spine as she looked inside. Right away, she could see something was missing. One of her red knee socks.

The one with the stolen jewels inside.

CHAPTER 13

Janie whirled around in shock.

"What's wrong?" Frederick asked.

"My bag," Janie said in a strangled voice. "Someone stole —"

Just then she heard little running footsteps. Janie looked up to see Violet scampering toward her, Mrs. Kayden hurrying behind.

Violet was clutching something in her hand.

"Janie! I found a scarf for our snowman!" she sang.

But it wasn't a scarf.

It was Janie's missing sock. Janie's blood ran cold as she saw the big bulge in the toe.

"Violet," Janie said, struggling to keep her voice calm. "I need that sock."

She gently took hold of the sock, plucking it from Violet's hand.

"Janie, no!" Violet screamed, snatching it back.

As the sock slipped from Janie's grip, the diamond jewels tumbled out. They seemed to hover in the air for a moment, like glittering stars.

Then they dropped to the floor with a loud clatter.

Janie froze, hardly believing what was happening.

"Come along," Mrs. Kayden said impatiently, taking Violet by the hand. Somehow, she hadn't noticed the jewels — baby Billy was squalling in her arms. "No more pestering Janie and Frederick."

"My snowman's scarf!" Violet cried as her mother pulled her away. "My snowman's scarf!"

Janie snapped into action. With shaking hands, she quickly gathered the jewels from the floor. But a big diamond ring was missing! Where could it have gone?!

She glanced all around, panic rising in her chest.

There it was! . . . Right on top of Frederick's boot. She reached for it, but Frederick beat her to it. He studied the ring in his hand while they both slowly stood up.

"Here you go," Frederick said, confusion flickering in his eyes as he handed her the ring.

But then he froze. And Janie watched as his expression changed from confusion to shock. His eyes widened, and his mouth dropped open.

His eyes moved from Janie to the ring and back again.

"Janie," he said, his voice barely a whisper. "Where did all these come from?"

Janie opened her mouth to answer, but no sound came out.

"Are they . . . are you . . . that man in the train station . . ."

Again, Janie tried to say something, but her voice had disappeared.

Frederick stared at her. "Are you a . . . thief?" He whispered the last word.

Lies swarmed into Janie's mind and lined themselves up on the tip of her tongue.

She looked at Frederick, really looked for the first time in all the days they'd been together. And she could see that he really did care about her. She swallowed the lies.

"I didn't steal them," she said, squeezing the jewels tight in her palm. "My job was just to take them on the train to Seattle."

Her voice wasn't bright and cheerful now. It was barely a whisper.

"There's a man named Ray Malvo. I work for him. Other kids do too. Orphans mostly. I don't have a grandmother. Or parents —"

Frederick's face started to change again, but Janie looked away. She knew he was disgusted with her. What was she thinking, spilling all this? Her heart clenched, like a fist closing tight.

Frederick didn't care about *her*. He cared about a girl who didn't exist. The polite girl. The respectable girl with manners and a cheerful smile.

Not the real Janie, the dirty criminal.

Janie had to get away — now. Before Frederick blabbed to his father and Miss Wade.

She turned and stuffed everything in her bag. She grabbed her coat.

And then without another word, she ran down the aisle of the empty sleeper car and out into the cold.

CHAPTER 14

She sprinted away from the train, ducked behind a snowdrift, and crept around to the back of the coal shed.

"Janie!"

Frederick had come after her.

"Janie!" he shouted.

Any minute he'd find his father. He'd tell Mr. McBride that Janie had been lying since the moment they met. Mr. McBride would be furious. Soon everyone on the train would know who she was. *What* she was.

A mob would come after her. And when they found her?

They'd lock her up somewhere — a shed, the freight car — until they could hand her over to the police.

Tick, tick, tick, tick.

Janie had to get away. But to where?

Tick, tick, tick, tick.

She closed her eyes, clearing her mind. She had to remember who she really was. Not some goody-goody little girl. Not a spoiled prince like Frederick. Janie had spent most of her life in the shadows. She knew how to hide. How to escape. How to disappear.

A plan quickly came to her: She'd walk to Scenic, then get on a train to Seattle. Just like Mr. Riggins had done.

She'd find a way to sell the jewels — she'd find a pawnshop somewhere — and then get to Boston. Just like she'd planned. But she couldn't leave for Scenic now. It was getting dark. She'd need to hide somewhere until the sun came up.

Bailets, she decided.

Supper hadn't started yet; only Mr. and Mrs. Bailets would be there right now. Janie would sneak in and find a place to tuck herself away for the night.

She peered around the coal shed. She didn't see — or hear — Frederick. He must have gone to the observation car to get his father and Miss Wade. She pictured their furious faces, their looks of horror and disgust. She closed her eyes again, wiping her mind clean.

Janie scurried up toward Bailets. She glimpsed Mr. and Mrs. Bailets through the dining room window. Ducking down, she made her way around the side of the building to a back door. In a flash, she was inside, hurrying past the kitchen.

She scanned for a place to hide. She heard footsteps — she had to move quickly.

She held her breath and rushed down the hall, carefully opening the first door she saw. It was a storage room filled with crates and barrels. Perfect. She squeezed behind a big barrel, settling herself in a dark corner. She lowered herself to the floor, pulling her knees tight to her chest.

It was pitch-dark in the room.

But Janie was used to the dark.

Tiny footsteps scratched around somewhere close. Rats, she was sure.

But Janie was used to rats.

Her stomach grumbled.

But Janie was used to being hungry.

Soon she heard muffled noises drifting from the dining room — voices, clinking dishes, scraping chairs. Supper had started. She pictured Frederick and Mr. McBride. Violet and her baby brother. Tears prickled behind Janie's lids. She squeezed her eyes closed, pushing the faces away.

Once, Mrs. Bailets opened the door to the storage room. She held her lantern as she grabbed a jar from a shelf and then left quickly.

The hours drifted by. The dining-room noises faded. Janie tried to sleep. She'd need plenty of strength for her long trek through the snow.

Finally, she managed to drift off, until, *Boom!*

Her eyes popped open. She was lying on the floor, curled up under an empty flour sack. It took her a moment to remember where she was.

Boom!

The jars on the shelves rattled.

Was that thunder? How much time had gone by? Could it be morning?

Janie wriggled out of her hiding place, stood up, and cracked open the door of the storeroom. She slipped out of the room and started down the hallway. Lightning flashed as she passed the kitchen. She caught a glimpse of the clock on the wall — one thirty-five in the morning.

It was still the middle of the night, hours before she could leave for Scenic. She heard the rain pouring down and more rumbles of thunder. *Strange*, she thought. She'd never heard of a thunderstorm after a blizzard. She hoped the rain stopped before morning.

She turned to go back to her hiding place. But then she heard noises coming from the dining room.

"We looked everywhere. But she's nowhere to be found."

Mr. McBride, for sure.

"We have to keep looking for her."

Frederick.

Janie crept closer, peering around a corner.

They were standing just inside the front door with Miss Wade and Mr. Bailets.

"She has to be somewhere in Wellington," Mr. McBride said. "There's no way she would have tried to walk to Scenic in the dark."

"I agree," Miss Wade said.

"She might have gotten into one of the shacks," Mr. Bailets said.

"This is all my fault!" Frederick said, his voice cracking.

His fault that Janie — the criminal — had escaped.

"It's not your fault," Miss Wade said.

"Let's go back to the train," Mr. McBride said, putting an arm around Frederick. "We'll keep looking in the morning."

Janie stepped back into the shadows.

She heard the front door open and footsteps head out. The last thing Janie heard before Mr. Bailets closed the door was Mr. McBride's voice.

"We'll find her. And I swear to you. I will not rest until that monster is in jail."

CHAPTER 15

Monster?

The word hit Janie like a kick in the guts.

But what did Janie expect? She'd lied. Tricked them all. Of course they hated her. She deserved it, she guessed.

She swallowed the lump in her throat and turned to go back to her hiding place, to wait out the night. But then Miss Wade's voice echoed in her mind.

It's not your fault.

She'd been talking to Frederick. So why did Janie feel like those words could have been meant for her?

A strange feeling — a hot jolt — shot up her spine.

"It's not my fault," she said softly. And then louder. "It's not my fault!"

"Who's there?" Mr. Bailets called out. But Janie didn't budge. Her mind was swirling.

All that had happened to her — losing her parents, living with Aunt Barbara, running from the police, hiding stolen jewels. She didn't choose any of it. She didn't *want* to be a criminal. She wanted to be the girl she was on the train, the girl who people trusted and cared about.

But . . . wait. Janie's eyes widened as a thought popped into her head. What if that girl *was* the real Janie?

And those people . . . her friends . . .

Could she make them understand? Would they maybe forgive her?

Before Janie realized what she was doing, she was rushing through the dining room. She flew past Mr. Bailets.

"Janie!" he called.

She pushed through the door and out into the rain.

Thunder boomed. Lightning slashed the sky. Rain poured down, mixing with the tears that streamed down Janie's cheeks. There they were up ahead — Mr. McBride and Miss Wade. And trailing behind them was Frederick. They were heading back toward the sleeper car.

"Wait!" Janie called. "Wait!"

Mr. McBride and Miss Wade didn't seem to hear. But Frederick turned.

"Janie!" Frederick exclaimed. He ran toward her. "We've been looking everywhere!"

Boom! Thunder shook the ground.

"I'm not a monster!" Janie cried.

"What?" Frederick said as a bolt of lightning lit up his face. He didn't look angry or disgusted with her. He looked relieved and sad and confused. But then he seemed to realize what Janie was talking about. He grabbed her hand and their eyes locked. "My father wasn't talking about you! He was talking about that evil man, Malvo."

In that moment, something deep inside Janie seemed to burst open. All those dark thoughts and feelings she'd been pushing away — the hurts and terrors, the tears, the questions, the memories . . . she couldn't hold them inside anymore.

She heard a strange sound.

Whump!

Her body shook. The ground trembled. A low roar filled her ears.

For a split second, Janie thought it was coming from *her*, from somewhere deep inside her bones.

But no.

"What was that?" Frederick said.

Janie spun around. She stared up at the mountain, which was brightly lit by a flare of lightning.

Except it didn't look like the same mountain. It seemed to have shattered apart. All the snow that had covered it was racing down the steep slope.

"It's an avalanche!" Frederick cried.

It was moving faster by the second, coming toward them. And toward the trains.

"Run!" Janie shouted.

She held tight to Frederick's hand as they sprinted back toward Miss Wade and Mr. McBride and up alongside the train.

"Wake up! Wake up!" they shouted.

They banged on the side of the cars as they raced along.

"Avalanche! Get out! Get out!"

But the sound of the avalanche was getting louder and louder, building into a roar that pounded Janie's ears.

Flashes of lightning lit up the sky. Janie could see the wave getting bigger, wider, faster.

Closer.

Closer.

She felt its icy breath huffing at their backs.

Suddenly the ground beneath their feet seemed to crumble. Janie's hand slipped from Frederick's. Her legs were pumping through the air. Snow and ice rose up around her. She felt she was being swallowed by a ferocious beast. Its massive jaws clamped down around her, its frozen teeth gripping her flesh.

It was eating her alive.

She was part of the avalanche now — and so were the train cars. They'd been lifted off the ground. Janie could hear them breaking apart all around her — wood shattering, metal shrieking and groaning, the steam engine hissing like a furious snake.

Fttttttt!

Ssssssss.

Cruuuuunch.

Snow swirled all around her. It raked her face, rushed up her nose, pummeled her body like hundreds of fists. Janie twisted and spun, neck whipping, legs and arms flailing, muscles tearing.

Worst of all, she couldn't breathe. For a split second, she felt a blast of air on her face. She opened her mouth and gulped in a breath before the icy jaws snapped shut again. Time seemed to slow, each second more painful than the last. She was sure her body would be torn apart, that her lungs would explode.

And then, suddenly, it all stopped. The noise. The motion. It seemed the entire world was holding its breath.

Janie lay there in complete blackness. She could see nothing. Hear nothing.

It was as though Janie — and the world — had disappeared.

CHAPTER 16

At first Janie wondered if she was even alive. But then white-hot panic shot through her body. *Breathe! Breathe!*

Her nose was jammed with snow. Her lips seemed frozen shut. Snow covered her face. There was just a sliver of space between her mouth and the icy mask of snow. She managed to sip in some small breaths. But this air wouldn't last long, she knew.

How deeply was she buried under the snow? What else lay on top of her? She pictured wrecked train cars. Boulders. Trees.

She tried moving her arms. But they were locked into place, like the snow was cement that had hardened around her. Her legs were stuck too.

She was buried alive.

She tried to scream, but she couldn't fill her lungs enough to make a sound. All that came out was a muffled moan. The weight of the snow seemed to be getting heavier, like a giant was stepping on her. Stomping on her chest. Crushing her bones. Pressing the air from her lungs.

It was hopeless, she thought. She'd never make it out of here alive. She was all alone. She felt herself disappearing into the dark. And maybe that's what she should do. For real.

And then came the sound of whispered words.

I think I can.

A tiny spark flared in Janie's mind.

I think I can.

Janie tried moving her arms again. Completely stuck. But wait — the thumb on her right hand. She wiggled it, twisted it, scraped the snow until there was more space. Enough so that now her index finger could move. She twisted her wrist, making more space.

I think I can.

She clawed harder with three fingers, then four. She balled her hand into a fist and pushed with all her might, twisting and turning, ignoring the pain of the snow ripping apart the skin on her knuckles. Her hand throbbed. Blood seeped.

I think I can.

She pushed harder — her whole arm was moving now, loosening the snow so that she could wiggle more of her body.

Her muscles throbbed.

I think I can.

Bit by bit, inch by inch, she kept pushing, until finally her hand punched through the surface. Raindrops splashed onto her fingers. She pushed her hand higher. Voices shouted. Someone grabbed hold of her hand, gripped her tight.

But by now Janie was barely breathing. Her mind had taken her far away from this snowy mountain wilderness. The whispering voice in her mind disappeared. She didn't hear the shouts of people frantically clearing away the snow and train wreckage that covered her. She didn't feel the strong arms lifting her up or gentle fingers brushing snow from her face.

It was many, many hours before she opened her eyes. And when she did, she was surprised to discover that she wasn't in a jail cell, or Aunt Barbara's apartment, or an icy grave beneath the snow.

She was in a soft bed, covered in warm blankets. She hadn't disappeared. And she wasn't alone.

Frederick was sitting by her bed, gripping her hand.

Wellington Avalanche Kills Nearly 100 People Deadly Disaster Shocks Nation

MARCH 10, 1910 | By Libby S. Wade

A deadly avalanche struck the town of Wellington, Washington, early in the morning on Tuesday, March 1. The exact number of dead is still not known, but estimates are close to one hundred. Most of the victims were passengers and crew from two Great Northern Railway trains.

The trains had been stranded for six days, trapped by a blizzard that dropped more than 30 feet of snow. The avalanche struck at approximately 1:40 A.M. on March 1, perhaps triggered by an unusual thunderstorm with heavy rains.

In seconds, the wave of snow had crushed buildings in Wellington. It then picked up the trains, broke them apart, and swept them off the cliff into a canyon 150 feet below the town.

Screams of terror echoed through the night as workers from Wellington rushed into the canyon to find survivors.

A mother and two children were pulled from the wreckage with mild injuries. Porter Louis Anderson survived being thrown from the train and rescued several members of the crew. A young boy was flung down the mountain but escaped injury. An eleven-year-old girl was found alive, buried under snow, fallen trees, and train debris.

But tragically, approximately thirty-five passengers plus dozens of crew members and railroad workers did not survive the disaster. One of the dead was J. L. Pettit, the beloved Great Northern Railway conductor.

At least one person has still not been found. At this point, their body may not be retrieved until warmer weather comes in the spring.

Already, the Great Northern Railway has promised to make changes in mountain train routes to protect trains from the danger of avalanches.

But for the families of those lost in Wellington, these changes come too late.

"Our family is heartbroken," says Leonard Letts, whose mother, seventy-five-year-old Mary Letts, died in the disaster. "But she will live on in the hearts of her children and grandchildren."

CHAPTER 17

THREE MONTHS LATER
JUNE 10, 1910
AROUND 3:00 P.M.
MASSACHUSETTS NORTHERN TRAIN

Chuggachuggachuggachugga.

Chuggachuggachuggachugga.

The train swayed gently as it sped along the tracks.

"Look!" Frederick said, pointing out the window next to Janie. "There it is! Right across the river!"

Janie stared out, her heart thumping with excitement.

100

"Beautiful city," said Mr. McBride, who was sitting just across the aisle.

"What a journey this has been," said the tall, bright-eyed woman next to him. She flashed a smile at Janie.

Mrs. McBride — Frederick's mother. It turned out she wasn't a spoiled rich lady at all. She was warm and kind. A little bit like Miss Eva.

Janie smiled back. *Yes*, she thought. *What a journey.* They'd left Seattle more than five days ago. They'd traveled three thousand miles, across the entire country.

But Janie's journey started way before this, she knew. Before she began this train trip with Frederick and his family . . . *her* family. She lived with the McBrides now. In their grand house in Seattle, overlooking the bay.

Some mornings she'd wake up, afraid that all of this was a dream. That she was back on the lumpy mattress on Aunt Barbara's floor. Or in a jail cell. Or in that frozen grave under piles of snow and wood and rocks.

But then she'd open her eyes, and there she'd be in her own sunny bedroom, with the flowered wallpaper and sunlight streaming through the big windows. She'd hear Frederick chattering away with his father and Mrs. McBride humming a pretty song.

What a journey.

And now here she was, about to arrive in Boston.

This trip had been all Mrs. McBride's idea, a way of celebrating Janie's twelfth birthday. "We have to meet this fellow you've told us so much about," Mrs. McBride had said.

Dash.

Mrs. McBride had gotten Dash's new address from Miss Eva, written to his cousins, and started planning this trip.

Janie pictured her old friend now — those flashing eyes, the brown curl that flopped over his forehead. She had so much to tell him! Where would she begin?

With Malvo, of course. He was in jail. Mr. McBride had gone to Spokane himself. He'd brought the stolen jewels to the police and hired a team of detectives to help them track Malvo down. He'd tried to find Aunt Barbara, to let her know Janie was safe. But Aunt Barbara had disappeared. She was probably afraid she'd wind up in jail too.

And of course, there was the avalanche.

Janie was sure Dash had already heard about the disaster — it made news all around the world. People said it was the deadliest avalanche in American history. And one of the worst train disasters too. Miss Wade had written at least ten articles about it. Now she was writing a whole book!

Janie had so many horrific memories, nightmares

of being buried alive. Sometimes she heard the echoes of people sobbing from their beds in those days after the disaster. She glanced down at her hands, at the scars on her fingers and knuckles.

But there had been some bright moments too, that Janie never wanted to forget. Like seeing Frederick sitting by her bed when she finally woke up. Meeting Mrs. McBride for the first time, how she'd hugged Janie like they were long-lost friends. And the day after the avalanche, when a little freckled face had appeared next to her bed.

"*Peekaboo*, Janie!"

Violet. That cute little pest had come through safe and sound. So had her mother and baby brother.

Chuggachuggachuggachugga.

Chuggachuggachuggachugga.

"There's the station!" Frederick exclaimed.

Janie's heart rose.

Was she really here?

She flashed back to that moment in February after Hammer was arrested. When it came to her — that she could escape. When those four words had popped into her mind.

I think I can.

Just four little words from that silly story about a talking steam engine. Was that really all it had taken to get Janie here? Just those four little words?

No, Janie knew.

She eyed Frederick and Mr. and Mrs. McBride. She thought of Miss Wade. She thought of all those people who had dug through the snow to rescue her. The nurses who had tended to her torn-up hands and broken ribs.

But those words had helped Janie start this journey. Kept her going when she was alone in the dark. Reminded her what she could do, who she really was.

Whooooooooo! Whooooooooo!

The train slowed. The brakes hissed.

"We're here!" Frederick exclaimed.

Janie looked out the window. She caught sight of her reflection. She saw a girl with bright and hopeful eyes. Sitting up strong. Smiling with excitement.

There I am, Janie thought.

That's me.

KEEP READING

to learn more about
the Wellington avalanche and
life in 1910.

REAL-LIFE WELLINGTON

Here are some photographs of the real-life places that inspired Janie's story.

The town of Wellington before the avalanche

The Hotel Bailets

The dining room at the Hotel Bailets. The woman on the right is the granddaughter of Mr. and Mrs. Bailets.

A snowy day in Wellington

A first-class sleeper car. The man in the background is a porter like Mr. Anderson.

Passengers play cards on a train similar to the Seattle Express No. 25.

A rotary plow and its crew at the Wellington station, around 1900

FINDING JANIE'S STORY

Dear Readers,

Kids often ask me which of my I Survived books was hardest to write. My answer: all of them!

Writing an I Survived book is, for me, like building a LEGO spaceship with thousands of pieces and no directions. I need to get all the pieces to fit together — facts from my research, insights from experts, characters from my imagination — to create a story that makes sense and that keeps you turning the pages. I want you to be fascinated by the history and science and to become friends with my characters.

All this takes months of work. There are times when I get very frustrated and worried. I'll realize that something is missing, some important part of the plot or character. And like a LEGO spaceship missing an important piece, my story starts to fall apart.

In those moments, I put my face in my hands and moan, "Noooooooooo!" (Luckily, nobody witnesses these sad scenes except my dog, Roy.)

This happened while I was writing this book. As I got to the later chapters, I could see that I was missing a very important piece. I had all the facts about Wellington. I had read fourteen books, many more articles, studied photographs and maps and videos. I had brought Janie to life and forged her friendship with Frederick. I'd worked out my plot — Malvo and the stolen jewels, Violet and the red sock, Janie's escape to Bailets, the avalanche crashing down.

But I was missing one small but magic ingredient.

If you've read some of my other I Survived books, you know that all of my characters have a source that provides them with jolts of inner strength and inspiration. It could be a memory of a beloved relative or a story or myth they've kept in their mind.

In *I Survived Hurricane Katina, 2005*, Barry was inspired by Akivo, a superhero he and his friend created for a comic contest. In *I Survived the Nazi Invasion, 1944*, Max finds strength in the Bible story about David and Goliath. Dexter, in *I Survived the Joplin Tornado, 2011*, often flashes back to his brother Jeremy, a Navy SEAL fighting in Afghanistan.

But where did Janie's inner inspiration come from? A song? A memory? A story? Nothing I tried seemed to work. Until I remembered a book I read to my four kids when they were young, *The Little Engine That Could*. It was the story about the little steam engine that chugged up a steep mountain, repeating the same words over and over. *I think I can. I think I can.*

Perfect!

Except it turned out that the book, by Watty Piper, wasn't published until 1930. That was twenty years after the Wellington disaster. So it seemed it wouldn't work. I put that idea aside.

But then I decided to do a little more digging. My eyes lit up as I discovered that the 1930 book was based on a story that was created in the early 1900s. Versions of it were widely told by teachers and in Sunday school classes. The whole point of the story was to inspire kids not to give up when they were struggling, to work hard, and to think in a positive way.

I sat back and pictured the librarian Miss Eva telling Janie and Dash that story. I imagined those words echoing through Janie's mind. I had found my missing piece.

It still took months of work to get that new magical ingredient to fit into my story. As I've told you, writing these books is really hard work. But I have help from my editor, Katie, who has taught me so much. And in the end all that work is worth it. Because I get to share these stories with you.

I hope Janie's journey inspires you in some way. And the next time you're feeling frustrated or worried or ready to give up, try whispering those four words to yourself — *I think I can*.

Of course, we need other people to help us. We need to work hard and not be afraid to make mistakes. But those four little words can be surprisingly powerful. They are for me!

THE LITTLE ENGINE THAT COULD

The title page illustration from an early copy of The Little Engine That Could

MORE FACTS

THE WELLINGTON DISASTER WAS NOT A NATURAL DISASTER

Humans didn't create the blizzard that dumped nearly thirty feet of snow over Wellington, Washington. Humans didn't cause that monstrous avalanche.

But humans decided to build train lines that crossed the Cascade Mountains — one of the most avalanche-prone places in America. Leaders of the Great Northern Railway knew that avalanches were a huge problem on that stretch of their train line. And yet they still decided to send two trains into those mountains during a ferocious blizzard.

Many people did blame the Great Northern Railway for the deaths of so many people. They particularly blamed the railroad's founder and leader, James J. Hill. Famously determined, Hill had been eager to stretch his railroad line across the Cascade Mountains. Once the line was built, he urged his teams to keep trains running no matter what. Late trains cost him money and hurt the reputation of his railroad.

But the Great Northern Railway was actually only one of three railroads that had lines crossing the Cascades. The other two lines happened to not have trains on the mountain that fateful night in 1910. And Hill and the Great Northern Railway workers had no way of knowing that they were sending those trains into a blizzard that would last for days. Today, technology helps us predict bad weather like blizzards and hurricanes and plan for them, often days in advance. Those tools didn't exist in 1910.

Also, passenger trains had crossed those mountains thousands of times since the line was built in 1893. Many trains had been stranded by "slides," including in 1907, when a passenger train was famously stuck for ten days, not too far from Wellington. But before the Wellington disaster, no passengers had ever lost their lives on that stretch of the Great Northern Railway.

When the two trains became stranded, workers for the Great Northern Railway worked around the clock to try to free them. But the snow came down too fast. The winds were too fierce. The Great Northern Railway leaders believed they had the power to conquer nature. But their mighty snowplows were no match for the awesome powers of the storm.

A newspaper report on the Wellington avalanche

THE TRAINS WERE HOPELESSLY TRAPPED

Imagine being stranded on a train in a ferocious blizzard, in a mountain wilderness at the edge of a cliff. You're surrounded by strangers. Day by day the snow gets deeper. Food runs low. The train starts to stink. And the whole time, you're watching as more and more snow builds up on the mountainside, hanging right above your train.

That's what the passengers and crew experienced during the six days leading up to the Wellington avalanche. Many passengers were terrified. They were haunted by the avalanche in Cascade that killed the workers Harry and John (they were real men who worked at the beanery).

Passengers could hear sounds of distant avalanches echoing through the mountains. Many knew in their bones that a terrible disaster was coming. I get chills thinking of this, how frightening it must have been!

Would I have been comforted by Mr. Bailets?

He really was convinced that Wellington was safe. Or would I have tried to escape to Scenic? Twelve men made that five-mile trek. They braved howling winds and chest-deep snow. One man was buried by a small avalanche and almost died.

The final stretch of the journey to Scenic was a trail that led down a steep mountainside into town. The trail was covered with snow and ice. The hikers had to slide down the mountain — 2,000 feet — sitting on their coats. Miraculously, they all made it.

I probably would have wanted to escape. But what if I had my kids with me? Or my eighty-two-year-old parents? Of course, I wouldn't have left them behind. I would have stayed on the train and surely shared the sense of doom many passengers felt as the hours ticked by.

Many passengers begged for the trains to be moved away from the cliff. That way, if an avalanche did hit, the trains wouldn't be thrown down into the canyon. But moving the trains wasn't possible. They were mostly buried by snow. The tracks were blocked by huge amounts of snow that rose up into enormous drifts. The plows had all broken down, and there were not nearly enough shovelers. In fact, most shovelers quit; they were paid only fifteen cents an hour, and the work was backbreaking.

What about moving the trains into the tunnel? That seemed like a good idea. But again, moving the trains wasn't possible. The tunnel was pitch-black and freezing cold. And what if an avalanche came down and trapped the trains *inside* the tunnel?

In the end, the trains were hopelessly trapped by a blizzard that would not let up.

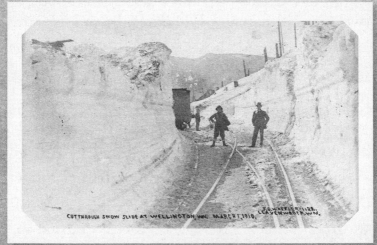

Walls of snow on either side of the tracks in Wellington

MOST PEOPLE DID NOT SURVIVE THE AVALANCHE

There were 125 people on the two trains that night. In addition to train passengers and crew, there were residents from town who had chosen to sleep in freight cars and on the mail train. These people mistakenly believed they'd be safer from avalanches on the train than in their flimsy shacks and bunkhouses in town. Ultimately, only twenty-three people from the trains survived.

In the minutes and hours following the avalanche, survivors and workers from the town rushed to help those buried and injured. Porter Louis Anderson (a real person) survived the avalanche and helped rescue several members of the train crew. One man hiked to Scenic in the pouring rain to summon help. In the following days, dozens of people arrived, including nurses and families of passengers and crew members.

Bad weather and the threat of avalanches made it difficult to find the bodies of those who were lost. In fact, the last body wasn't found until July, twenty-one weeks after the disaster.

A train car in the Wellington avalanche wreckage

Rescue workers drag bodies from the avalanche back to town.

THE WELLINGTON DISASTER
LED TO CHANGES

Within weeks of the disaster, Great Northern Railway founder James Hill promised to make it safer to travel by train through the Cascades. Over the next few years, the railroad constructed more snowsheds — roofs over the tracks to protect trains from avalanches.

But these new snowsheds didn't prevent additional train disasters from avalanches. During the winter of 1915–1916, record amounts of snow fell in the Cascades. Three avalanches hit passenger trains that year, killing a total of fifteen people and injuring dozens.

The biggest change didn't happen until 1929, when the new Cascade Tunnel was completed. At nearly eight miles long, it was the longest tunnel in the Western Hemisphere. It enabled trains to pass far more safely through the mountains, completely avoiding the most dangerous stretches near Wellington. This tunnel is still in use today.

Workers build the new Cascade Tunnel, 1926.

RAILROADS CHANGED THE UNITED STATES — IN GOOD WAYS AND BAD

Before the late 1800s, traveling over long distances was slow and often dangerous. There were no cars, no highways, no airplanes. Just traveling a few miles could take hours on a horse or by boat. A trip across the country took at least five months. Thousands of people died on grueling cross-country journeys by horse and buggy.

No wonder many people lived their whole lives without leaving their small towns.

Railroads changed all that. The first railroads started chugging in the 1860s. By the early 1900s, Americans were connected by hundreds of different railroad lines that stretched into most corners of the country. Friends and relatives could stay connected. Millions of people moved west. New kinds of businesses boomed. Sleepy towns like Seattle became bustling cities.

But there was a tragic side to the growth of railroads. As more railways were built and more people moved west, members of Native American nations and tribes — men, women, and children — were robbed of their lands, their traditions, and in some cases, even their lives.

The men who owned the railroads also cared little about their workers. Most of those who built the railroads were immigrants, men from China, Ireland, and Italy. They suffered prejudice, were paid little, and risked their lives clearing forests, blasting through mountains, and building tracks. Thousands of these laborers were killed or injured on the job. The same was true for the men who worked on the trains — the engineers, conductors, and brakemen.

I was stunned to learn how dangerous train travel was in those days. And it wasn't only avalanches that threatened trains. Steam engines exploded. Trains sped out of control off mountainsides, tumbled off bridges, and crashed into other trains, motorcars, and people. The Wellington disaster actually isn't the deadliest *train* disaster in US history. In 1918, a train crash in Brooklyn, New York, killed some 100 people.

Gradually, laws were passed to protect workers. New technologies have made trains safer and reduced the number of accidents. There are still some train accidents every year in the United States and around the world. But overall, trains are among the safest ways to travel.

Turn the page to see photos of ways railroads affected America — both the good and bad.

A 1915 advertisement for shipping company Wells Fargo & Co Express, highlighting how quickly trains could deliver mail cross country.

ACROSS THE CONTINENT

Once 32 days
Now 4 days

THE FARGO WAY

A 1900 first-class lounge car (also known as an observation car) on the Northern Pacific Railway, complete with electric lights

An 1876 first-class train ticket from the Central Pacific Railroad Company

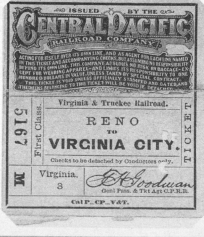

ISSUED BY THE

CENTRAL PACIFIC
RAILROAD COMPANY

ACTING FOR ITSELF OVER ITS OWN LINE, AND AS AGENT FOR EACH LINE NAMED IN THIS TICKET AND ACCOMPANYING CHECKS, BUT ASSUMING NO RESPONSIBILITY BEYOND ITS OWN LINE. THIS COMPANY ASSUMES NO RISK ON BAGGAGE—EXCEPT FOR WEARING APPAREL—AND LIMITS ITS RESPONSIBILITY TO ONE HUNDRED DOLLARS IN VALUE, UNLESS TAKEN BY SPECIAL CONTRACT. THIS TICKET IS VOID UNLESS OFFICIALLY STAMPED AND DATED, AND THE CHECKS BELONGING TO THIS TICKET WILL BE VOID IF DETACHED.

Virginia & Truckee Railroad.

5167

First Class.

RENO
TO
VIRGINIA CITY.

TICKET

Checks to be detached by Conductors only.

M

Virginia.
8

EH Goodman
Genl Pass. & Tkt Agt C.P.R.R.

Cal P.—CP.—V&T.

Chinese laborers build a stretch of the Northern Pacific Railroad in Montana. About 1,500 Chinese workers helped complete the job. It was backbreaking, dangerous work.

Train crashes like this 1887 crash outside Chatsworth, Illinois, were common. This disaster killed eighty-five people and injured hundreds more.

JANIE IS BASED ON REAL CHILDREN FROM 1910

I wish I could say that Janie is fictional, that she sprang from my imagination. Sadly, that is not true. During the late 1800s and into the early 1900s, thousands of American children were orphans or came from families who weren't able to take care of them. At that time, if a parent lost a job or got sick, they had nowhere to turn for help. That's why so many children ended up in orphanages or in terrible situations like Janie's.

Visitors to cities like New York and Chicago were horrified by the sight of children begging on the streets, sleeping in alleys, and roaming in gangs of pickpockets and thieves. It was not uncommon for kids to wind up working for gangs led by criminals, like Ray Malvo. He is a fictional character but based on real people I discovered in my research.

By the early 1900s, more was being done to help these children. Laws were passed to help families in need and to better protect children. Today, a child like Janie would have many people to help her.

In some ways, the character of Janie is similar to Jennie, a character who appears in *I Survived the Great Chicago Fire, 1871*. In that book, Jennie is an orphan trying to take care of her little brother, Bruno, working for a gangster to earn money for food. She's fierce and proud and helps main character Oscar escape the flames devouring the city.

But I always wanted to make Jennie — or a character just like her — a main character. And so I transported her to 1910, to the state of Washington, and took her on a journey of her own.

Street children around 1900

AVALANCHES ARE AMONG THE MOST POWERFUL FORCES IN NATURE

A large avalanche can weigh one million tons (that's about the same as 500,000 cars). A typical avalanche races down a mountain at about 60–80 miles per hour. These events — also called snowslides — happen with little warning. One minute you're looking at a beautiful snowy mountainside. The next minute there's a raging wave of churning snow heading right for you.

Why do avalanches happen? In the mountains, layers of snow build up over weeks and months. Each layer of this snowpack has a different texture. Some layers are thick, some are thin. Some are icy, some are mushier. As more and more snow piles on top, the weaker layers underneath can start to break. At that point, the slightest weight — a person skiing or snowboarding, the footsteps of a hiker — can send the whole snowpack crashing down the mountain.

In a typical year, there are hundreds of thousands of avalanches in mountain ranges around the world. Luckily, only a few of these happen where there are people nearby. Still, about 150 people around the world are killed by avalanches each year. Most are skiers, snowboarders, or people riding snowmobiles.

It is very unlikely that you would ever get caught in an avalanche, especially if you follow these simple rules:

• When you are skiing or snowboarding in a mountain area, always stay on the trail. Do not

An avalanche in Russia

An avalanche warning sign

ski out of bounds. Ski resorts in avalanche-prone areas work to protect skiers from avalanches. They even set off small explosions to purposely trigger avalanches — before skiers are on the trails. Always pay attention to warnings.

- If you live in a mountainous area, use caution when hiking or snowmobiling after a large amount of snow has fallen. Strong winds are another risk factor for avalanches, and so is a sudden rise in temperature. Never venture out on your own.

TODAY, WELLINGTON IS A GHOST TOWN

In fact, it's not even called Wellington. A few months after the disaster, the railroad changed the name of the town to Tye (after the Tye River, which runs below the town). After the new Cascade Tunnel was completed, the Great Northern Railway shut down the town and others around it. Workers pulled up the tracks and boarded up the buildings. What they left behind has mostly rotted away or disappeared behind trees and weeds.

Today, people do visit the area to hike the Iron Goat Trail, which takes hikers along the old railroad bed. You can still see hunks of wreckage jutting from the ground and the old Cascade Tunnel, which some believe is haunted.

There is a metal plaque that dedicates the trail to those who built the train line and those who lost their lives "through accidents and avalanche disasters."

Hikers enter the Cascade Tunnel on the Iron Goat Trail.

SELECTED BIBLIOGRAPHY

America's Worst Train Disaster: The 1910 Wellington Tragedy, by Don Moody, Abique, 1998

Conquest and Catastrophe: The Triumph and Tragedy of the Great Northern Railway Through Stevens Pass, by T. Gary Sherman, AuthorHouse, 2004

The Great Northern Railway: A History, by Ralph W. Hidy, Muriel E. Hidy, Roy V. Scott, and Don L. Hofsommer, University of Minnesota Press, 1988

Iron Empires: Robber Barons, Railroads, and the Making of Modern America, by Michael Hiltzik, Houghton Mifflin Harcourt, 2020

Northwest Disaster: Avalanche and Fire, by Ruby El Hult, Binfords & Mort, 1960

Rails Across the Cascades, by Eva Anderson, World Publishing Company, 1989

"Snow Fall: The Avalanche at Tunnel Creek," by John Branch, *The New York Times*, December 20, 2012, also available online at https://www.nytimes.com/projects/2012/snow-fall/index.html

Stevens Pass: Gateway to Seattle, by JoAnn Roe, Caxton Press, 2002

The White Cascade: The Great Northern Railway Disaster and America's Deadliest Avalanche, by Gary Krist, Henry Holt and Company, 2007

PHOTO BY DAVID DREYFUSS

Lauren Tarshis's *New York Times* bestselling I Survived series tells stories of young people and their resilience and strength in the midst of unimaginable disasters and times of turmoil. Lauren has brought her signature warmth, integrity, and exhaustive research to topics such as the September 11 attacks, the American Revolution, Hurricane Katrina, the bombing of Pearl Harbor, and other world events. Lauren lives in Connecticut with her family, and can be found online at laurentarshis.com.